CASE FILES

UNSOLVED

Authors Of The Future

Edited By Sarah Waterhouse

First published in Great Britain in 2021 by:

Young Writers
Remus House
Coltsfoot Drive
Peterborough
PE2 9BF
Telephone: 01733 890066
Website: www.youngwriters.co.uk

Book Design by Ashley Janson

Softback ISBN 978-1-80015-508-4

Printed and bound in the UK by BookPrintingUK
Website: www.bookprintinguk.com
YB0476P

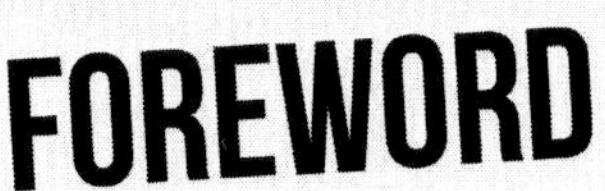

FOREWORD

As long as there have been people, there has been crime, and as long as there have been people, there have also been stories. Crime fiction has a long history and remains a consistent best-seller to this day. It was for this reason that we decided to delve into the murky underworld of criminals and their misdeeds for our newest writing competition.

We challenged secondary school students to craft a story in just 100 words on the theme of 'Unsolved'. They were encouraged to consider all elements of crime and mystery stories: the crime itself, the victim, the suspect, the investigators, the judge and jury. The result is a variety of styles and narrations, from the smallest misdemeanors to the most heinous of crimes. Will the victims get justice or will the suspects get away with murder? There's only one way to find out!

Here at Young Writers it's our aim to inspire the next generation and instill in them a love of creative writing, and what better way than to see their work in print? The imagination and flair on show in these stories is proof that we might just be achieving that aim! The characters within these pages may have to prove their innocence, but these authors have already proved their skill at writing!

CONTENTS

Stephenson Academy, Stantonbury

Ummul Mumineen Academy, Grangetown

THE STORIES

IMMORTALITY SERUM

People think the dead can't talk; but when you're being chased by a man you just killed, you begin to think a little differently. Blue liquid dribbles from his mouth, landing on a smashed beaker embossed with the logo. A round of bullets hit the man. He crumples.

"Cut!"

Thousands in debt, we're supposed to get this right.

"Next."

I sigh. We can't afford to keep them alive any longer. The next subject stumbles in. Once we get this right, these lives lost will be worth it. The needle pushes the mixture under the skin. *Bang! Bang!* The subject stands...

Emily Kelt (15)
Craigmount High School, Edinburgh

HOW TO GET AWAY WITH MURDER

"Guilty or innocent, how do you plead?"
"Innocent." I was lying; a skill considered invaluable in this profession. While dealing with the unpleasantries in the courtroom, I uncovered the mistake that almost cost me my life. The darn gloves. A note to those desiring to enter this profession: clean-up is key. As for my time in the courts, there is a great book by Remi Chauveux that contains some of the best alibis in the business. Another essential piece of equipment is a pair of treadless shoes, useful for sneaking around places you may wish to procure valuable items from...

Fraser Petrie (15)
Craigmount High School, Edinburgh

JUST A DREAM

It was just a dream.

One night, years ago, I killed a man out of rage. I immediately felt regret. What if I were caught?

Waking up was a relief, a weight lifted off my shoulders. The next night, I returned to face the aftermath of my awful crime. I was arrested, stood trial and was sentenced to life in prison.

This wasn't just one night. It was an episode of nightmares over and over that I returned to repeatedly. I tried forcing myself to stay awake in order to avoid the inevitable, but eventually I lost. Was it real?

Sophie Rutherford (14)

Craigmount High School, Edinburgh

THE DARK SHADOW

A scary black shadow always appears late at night in the woods. One time, someone tried to find that scary, malicious shadow looming around in the woods. People say that it has a killing streak of two thousand. The woman who was trying to find it is called Alissa Floyde. She is very brave. Eventually, after thirteen years, she finally found the shadow. She snuck up on it and pounced on its back. She took the dark hood off, but no one was under it. She thought, *it's a ghost!* She will never know whose shadow it was...

Eve Ward (12)
Craigmount High School, Edinburgh

BOATING ACCIDENT

"SpongeBob!" Patrick exclaimed as SpongeBob was hit in a boating accident. Or, was it planned? It was the fish Mafia; SpongeBob must not have paid them. He was in debt. As SpongeBob was on the floor as flat as a pancake, Patrick was sobbing.

After three weeks, Patrick had no reason to live. Patrick ended his life and became a souvenir in the Bikini Bottom beach store above the water. But SpongeBob woke up from a coma. He had no injury as he was a sponge! After finding out Patrick took his life, SpongeBob decided to...

Finlay Allan (14)
Craigmount High School, Edinburgh

GUILTY

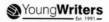

"Guilty!" the judge said. I'd been wrongfully accused while the real killer was roaming free. My life felt as if it was coming to an end. The prison guards came, they put the handcuffs on so tight to the point my hands were turning blue. They put me in a van with no windows, metal walls and a cage door separating me from the guards. I couldn't stop thinking that the real killer was free - free to do whatever he wanted to do. I had to escape. I couldn't bear the thought of serving forty years behind bars. Help!

Tony Harrison (14)
Craigmount High School, Edinburgh

THE NOTE

Dr Gray woke up at night to get a drink when, suddenly, a black figure swooped in, dragging him away.
The next day, Dr Gray's twenty-nine-year-old son came to visit and found a note saying: 'If you would like your dad back, go to the nearest park with £25,000. If you fail you'll never see your dad again'.
When he arrived at the park, he saw two men, one was his father. The son had not brought the money, instead he brought the police. The man walked over and was immediately arrested and unmasked...

Adam Sandeman (13)
Craigmount High School, Edinburgh

MCDONALD'S AND BAD GUY

One day, I went to McDonald's and there was a scary man at the door. He started following me, so I ran as fast as I could but he ran after me. So, I began running towards the police station. When I arrived, he'd run away. I told the police and I went back to McDonald's to get my food because I was hungry. After I got it, I ran super fast home and ate my McDonald's. My parents got home and I told them the story while eating my McDonald's because I was hungry. Luckily, it was not cold.

Fin Connolly (12)
Craigmount High School, Edinburgh

MUM DIED?

"Guilty!" the judge spoke. This was bad, real bad. If I never find the evidence then my life will be ruined.
I found the clue, everything my life relied on was right in front of me. I stood there, the knife with blood on it in front of me. I knew who did it, but I just couldn't snitch on them. If I did, I think it would still lead back to me. I mean, obviously it would. The only person near my mum when she was murdered was me, but I knew where my father was, close by...

Cara Duffus Short (14)
Craigmount High School, Edinburgh

FRIDAY THE 13TH

My name is Jack. Today is Friday the 13th, the unluckiest day of the year. The day started like any other day. I got up, had breakfast, cleaned my teeth, the usual. But something was wrong. My brother had the same feeling.
Then it hit me, my mum... I hadn't seen her all day. We were supposed to go to my dad's house today, but she was not there to take us. We walked there, the door was locked. My brother suggested to go round the back.
My mum was dead. Dad shot her!

Oliver Martindale (12)
Craigmount High School, Edinburgh

THE BREAK-IN

It is eleven at night, all is dark. Tonight's the night I am going to break into the bank. Here is my plan: I am going to walk in and hide in the spare room until it closes, then it will be time. I'm going to sneak around, being careful not to trip the alarm. I already made a copy of the keys to get into the safe where they keep all the money. I want to steal around twenty thousand pounds to help my mum pay for things because money is tight, Wish me luck.

Emily Skeldon (12)
Craigmount High School, Edinburgh

UNSOLVED

"Guilty!"
Clyde Blossoms pleaded guilty for the murder of Alfie Quinn.
The night the murder happened, Alfie Quinn was wearing a red velvet cloak with an apple in his hand. He was murdered brutally with a hatchet attached to a kitchen knife smashed into his skull. The murder happened at 11pm on Thursday night in Cooper Land Park.
Clyde was sentenced to Minsvile Prison.

Alfie Dymock (12)
Craigmount High School, Edinburgh

ASSASSINATION

We slid in silently, the starless sky eating away any shadows made. The King slept soundly, oblivious to his death knell waiting to ring. With serpentine stealth, we slithered towards him. Her hand crept towards me, her body poised to attack.

But we were not silent enough.

He leapt up, pinning us against his solid body.

"Long live the King," the Prince whispered vehemently. As the lifeless Assassin fell, joining the corpse of the King, the Prince wiped my cool tip stained with my master's blood on a handkerchief, fastening me in his weapon's belt.

"You're mine now, Little Knife."

Hebah Patel (15)

Crown Hills Community College, Leicester

THEY DESERVED THIS

Dripping with their crimson blood, the knife in my hand stared at me, pleading and begging for another taste. I grinned at it, recasting my gaze towards the carcasses spread out on the kitchen floor, which caused my smile to instantly intensify. They deserved this. Their bodies stayed satisfyingly still, a sight for sore eyes. The sound of sirens slowly approached and halted outside the house. They deserved this. Officers smashed the door down and saw me lying on the floor, recovering from unconsciousness, dazed and confused, muttering the words, "Mum...? My brothers...? What happened to them? Who did this?"

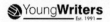

Ismat Jusab (15)
Crown Hills Community College, Leicester

UNSOLVED

Silence. He finally stopped his incessant whining. His blood oozed onto the carpet, creating a crimson shadow of the man he once was. The dark flame in my gut calmed, no longer ferocious enough to render me restless. I could sleep peacefully now. It was over.
Sirens blared in my ears. Time was up. I closed my eyes and smiled, inhaled and exhaled. Blood - not mine - smeared across my hands and face, painting a picture words could never describe. Its warmth brought me an inexplicable joy.
His blood.
Laughing, I raised my hands in surrender. It was truly over.
Silence.

Halima Miah (15)
Crown Hills Community College, Leicester

THE PSYCHOPATH

Some may call me sadistic, but that's just the cherry on top.
I see, you're a mutilated corpse on the floor. I might've been an unbidden visitor - but my egregious actions are not of your concern. Like you said, I have an affable demeanour, but one wrong move - I become very stern.
Can you hear that? The police are on their way. You suspect, as a culprit, I'd be running away. But it's all under control; forensics have nothing on me. You helped me with that.
Raucous fists bang on the door.
"It's the police! Let us in!"
It's showtime!

Mahfuzah Ali (14)
Crown Hills Community College, Leicester

THE TALE OF THE MAN WHO ATE BRICKS

A shadow at the door... "Confession is over!" bellowed across the chamber. He'd found me. I bundled myself through the window and charged towards my getaway vehicle. The screech of the tyre, the splutter of the engine and I was off. Or so I thought, until a heap of bricks came raining down on my car.

I was surrounded by darkness. In front of me, the priest-turned-hitman. "Make my hydrogen bomb!" He grabbed a handful of bricks and shoved it down my gullet.

"Never!" To make it was to live. To not was to suffer a painful, merciless death...

Owais Darwesh (15)
Crown Hills Community College, Leicester

MALEGATIE'S CURSE

It just didn't add up. We had hit another dead end. Gazing out of the window, I wondered who'd die next. "Malegatie's curse of two kids, so be..." I stared cluelessly...
Mia wakes me out of my daydream. "Come on, Azka." I pack away, the lifeless soul and pool of blood in front of me. Something in the shadows catches my attention. Hallucinating again, realisation hits me... Malegatie was the witch who killed my parents, who were the rightful protectors of Leicesterwood, and my brother is next. I must save my people before it's too late!

Azka Jonaid (15)
Crown Hills Community College, Leicester

THE LAST ACT

Killed. Murdered. Who knows? No one. I walk freely. Slowly. Nobody will know it's me! The dead can't talk... I'm safe. I've left the dead body. Eyes closed. Arm hanging. On my way home, a smirk creeps up on my face. I sleep.

The next day, I'm awake. On my way to work. "Detective Sally! Murder!" They'll never know.

"I know... The victim was killed by a knife!" I say. I walk away to think. I've won. They've lost. The power of the police is in my hands. Today, they will all be dead. Tomorrow, I will be gone. Forever.

Shifa Ashfak (13)
Crown Hills Community College, Leicester

THE UNPREDICTABLE MURDER

As she was approaching the terrifying alleyway, she started to doubt everything she had done. The situation was getting out of hand and now she needed to cover up this unfaithful crime. She never thought she would do this, but she had no choice but to listen to the psychopath who elegantly *forced her* to murder. She had to hide the lifeless figure in the basement and was threatened that she would be next if she informed the police. Guilt boiled inside her, seeing her parent's unconscious body lying on the cold floor. "I hate you... Mom."

Mira El Shazly (13)
Crown Hills Community College, Leicester

ONE SHOT

I don't always do what I'm told, but this time... I had to deliver this package in the middle of the mall, so said the mysterious person who called me this morning. I was told that even if I dropped the package once, I'd get killed. I was scared, but carried on. My hands shook, people passing by stared at me. They probably thought I was a weirdo. I wanted to tell one of them, but stopped myself. I carried on walking until I hit a rock and fell. I heard a shot. I opened the package and was shot...

Jashandeep Singh (13)
Crown Hills Community College, Leicester

UNSOLVED

My chest hurt from screaming. "I didn't do it! I have an alibi!"
Nothing. Silence. I was being dragged, footsteps echoing throughout the dark hall. My feet were scraping against the floor like sandpaper, my shoulder in intense pain. *Thud!* A door swung open. I was thrown onto a freezing floor. I couldn't feel my arm. Was it even there? I crawled around, searching for something. Anything. But it was just me. Fear started creeping in. What do these people want from me? *Hum!* I jumped. A blinding light was staring me right in the face.
"You did it!"

Molly McCrum (15)
Glengormley High School, Newtownabbey

GOING ON A WALK ALONE ISN'T ALWAYS A PLEASURE

One day, a teenage girl called Hannah went adventuring in a lively forest. It seemed like she was walking forever when she was met with an unforgiving storm. The clouds were darker than her thick black hair. Hannah had always struggled with PTSD, so the thunderstorm brought back painful memories of 'that' day. Suddenly, there was a hissing voice that echoed in the howling wind, then she saw it... The dark unsightly figure lurking behind a tree. As Hannah got closer, it disappeared in a lightning strike. She got whacked in the head. All she remembers is a dragging sensation...

Hannah Douglas (14)
Glengormley High School, Newtownabbey

DID I?

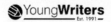

No comment! It wasn't me! The door slammed and I was alone. Thousands of thoughts running through my mind. Sweat dripping from my forehead. My memory was blurry from that gruesome night weeks ago, but I wouldn't even think about doing something as twisted as that.
Days went by where I ate slush, did my work and slept, but I still couldn't remember what happened. Then it hit me. The little girl being dragged through the woods, the menacing laugh and the screams of the child. The torture, TV reports and grieving family. That's when I realised... I did it!

Sophie Mackenzie (15)
Glengormley High School, Newtownabbey

UNSOLVED

Holding my breath, I hear the police bust down my house door. They search every room as I hide in my eerily silent cellar. Sawdust falls on my head from in-between the floorboards. I think of all the things that have happened. *I didn't do it*, I think, *so why does only one person believe me?* All those people, all those families ruined, and for what? The door creaks open, I'm as still as a statue... My bewildered best friend stands in the doorway and shoots... Dragging my lifeless body to the cops, getting away scot-free to unleash hellfire...

Jay Crosbie (15)
Glengormley High School, Newtownabbey

UNSOLVED

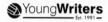

Everything's gone blank. I feel the rumble of the wall and floors, going straight up through my spine. I thought this was all a dream... until the dream turned into reality. I open my eyes. This cold Tuesday night in Liverpool hits me. This isn't the moment. This isn't an unsolved dream. All my hard work has brought me here. This is my time. This is my time to walk out.
"Come on, the lads!" Loud whistles from thousands of people almost burst my eardrums. Life doesn't feel real. *Is this just a computer game? Please be reality!*

Stephen Crumlin (15)
Glengormley High School, Newtownabbey

THE UNSOLVED CASE OF DB COOPER

As we jumped out the plane, we lost every single trace of him. All we had was a crude sketch and the tie he took off before jumping with the parachute, one of his demanded items for safe return of the hostages. Along with the chute, the suspect had demanded immunity and $200,000 in unmarked and untraceable bills. How long had he thought this through? It seemed he must've done for a long time. We met his demands, of course, as they were reasonable enough and we also believed we could catch him, but we didn't... Leaving the case unsolved.

Jake Smith (15)
Glengormley High School, Newtownabbey

UNSOLVED

It just didn't add up. I mean, how could I be sitting on the electric chair, on Death Row, awaiting death? "Guilty! Guilty! Guilty!" is what's being chanted at me as I sit on this death device, gazing at the crowd, their icy glares piercing through my soon-to-be-burnt-to-a-crisp body. I can smell the fear radiating off my body as they place the hood over my teary eyes. I'm afraid of the dark, more so than death itself. The cheers of the crowd muffle as I welcome death with open arms, consumed by darkness forever...

Aimee Wisdom (15)
Glengormley High School, Newtownabbey

DREAMS OR REALITY?

I see them, I see them when I sleep, when I haven't slept. My mind is like an everlasting loophole, flashing from life to life. Each night, I'm the new victim. The next day, it's on the news. I've been man, woman and child. I've lived with the horror of each victim, heard their thoughts, spoken their words. Every detail stays in my mind as clear as day; why don't I remember their faces?

Last night, I gave up and slept. I awoke in my dream. I was me... Was I the next victim? Then I saw my bloody hands...

Katie Hagan (15)

Glengormley High School, Newtownabbey

UNSOLVED

Unsolved. The mystery was still unsolved. Ever since the day his body was found, April had been a wreck. She wondered who killed him, where they'd done it and why. Why did they choose him? He was innocent. April's thoughts drove her crazy. She was always on edge. She tried to hide the fact she was struggling by going on walks around the park with family, but every so often you'd notice a single tear falling onto her rosy cheeks. We tried to reassure her that he was watching down on her and he would want her to be happy.

Hannah McWilliams (15)

Glengormley High School, Newtownabbey

JOHN SMITH

On the 5th of May, 2021, on a warm summer's day, John Smith was sent to prison. He has been charged with first-degree murder and kidnapping. He started with his own family, locking them in the garage, scared, cold and confused at what Dad's was doing. He shot all of them, even his daughter Rose. She was a sweet girl. Who knew giving the press a name would make it go on the most-wanted list? As he screamed that he was being framed whilst the judge ignored him, I left the courtroom a new man, John Smith.

Travis Taylor (15)
Glengormley High School, Newtownabbey

UNSOLVED

There I was, sat cold and alone in a tight, small and rough prison cell for the crime I 'didn't even do'. I was starved for days to try and get that information out of me that I 'didn't have'. As the days went on, I started to get used to the prison and its brutal food. It was like a school canteen but ten times worse.
A month later, I only had three weeks left in jail. I had made some new friend whilst spending time in jail. That's the story of when I robbed the cornershop.

Jude Molyneaux (15)
Glengormley High School, Newtownabbey

LOST BUT NOT FOUND

As I'm locking the cafe after my shift, a shadow moves in front of the door. I leave out the back door. A black SUV follows me down the street. As I turn around, a dark intimidating figure stands in front of me. Then, as a cloth is put to my mouth, all I see is darkness.
I stir awake, blinded by the sun. I jolt out of bed, realising one thing. I was kidnapped! The door bursts open, in walks a man. I assume my kidnapper. As I look at him, I wonder, *will he ever set me free?*

Maisie Hutton (14)
Glengormley High School, Newtownabbey

UNSOLVED

I tried to help them, I really did! Never did I think I would have to spend a Saturday in court, let alone my whole life in jail. They were so vulnerable, anyone could have done it, but who would hate me so much that they would frame me for murder? I would never hurt two little girls. Now their bodies lie and their parents are sobbing, blaming me. What will my family say? Will they believe me? The judge has all the evidence that it was me. It feels so realistic that maybe I did do it...

Emily Bremner (13)
Glengormley High School, Newtownabbey

SOLVED...?

I am a murderer. I murdered my wife in cold blood ten years ago today. There isn't a second that goes by where I don't think about what I've done. I love my wife, at least I did, so why would I do this? How could I murder the only person I've ever loved? When did my love stop? When did her love stop? She loves me, at least she did, up until I murdered her of course, or maybe even before that, but she loved me all the same. She loved me, so why would I have murdered her?

Kira Jamison (15)
Glengormley High School, Newtownabbey

UNSOLVED

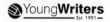

The suspect was gone...
Zainab, Saqlain and I huddled together back to back in a state of shock.
"Should we separate?" asked Saqlain with a stutter.
"Sure," Zainab replied. "Make sure not to let him escape."
As we were about to leave the room... "And make sure to be careful," Zainab interrupted. We nodded and spread out.
We were on a group call, something sounded wrong... I froze when I saw the picture frame. Where were our parents? They were in this image earlier! Laughter spread across the room, a man's voice.
"Is everything okay?" asked Saqlain. I didn't answer...

Zainab Aslam (13)
Mount St Joseph Business & Enterprise College, Farnworth

YOUNG BLOOD

"Up, down, up, down, all together now, Mr Clown is coming to town! Murdering children is what I do, watch out, I might come for you!"
"Mr Teddy, you plead guilty for murdering twenty-five children and parents. Is this true?"
"How about you ask them yourself?"
"Wait ... They're dead. Mr Teddy, you are charged with the death penalty for murdering twenty-five children and parents at a party."
The room goes dark and cold. A sudden gust of wind passes by. My Teddy's nowhere to be seen. People say he's on the run... What do you think? Watch out, children!"

Aliesha Nturo (12)
Mount St Joseph Business & Enterprise College, Farnworth

EVIL JUSTICE FOR INNOCENCE

"Guilty! Guards, get this poor person out of here."
"Wait, Your Honour, listen to me!"
"Nah, get the hell out, you're denied bail until you die. You're smoked so you are gonna pay the darn price."
"But why, sir?"
"Are you dumb?"
"No!"
"Ya know what? Execute him!"
"Execute me and God will make you die."
"Well, who's the judge? Me or you... the poor, stinky person?"
"Me?"
"Get the hell out! Guards, execute him!"

Sameer Bakhtar (12)
Mount St Joseph Business & Enterprise College, Farnworth

MASKED MURDERER

People think the dead can't talk, but I'm about to prove everybody wrong. The spirits of my victims talk to me. Hopefully you'll be next for me!
"Let me out, untie me right now!"
"No, my dear child. I ain't gonna kill you, I'll just torture you. Ha ha ha!"
"No, please, I beg for mercy!"
"If you don't lower your volume, you shall end up like all the other children, with my fellow community. There will be no way out."
I storm out. The kids growl in the basement...

Maja Och (12)
Mount St Joseph Business & Enterprise College, Farnworth

THE FAKED DEATH

At 4:05pm, police cars had surrounded the area. Thousands in confusion... On the floor, I saw a body. It was covered with crime scene tape. The murderer had escaped. The case was closed.
Thirty years later, on my way to work, I had accidentally collided with a person. This wasn't any ordinary person. I recognised the face. Suddenly, I remembered. It was the same face: James Parker. The death case that had been forgotten. Had he reincarnated? Or was his death fake?
I still look back at that day, trying to solve this unsolved mystery...

Rukhma Rahim (11)
Mount St Joseph Business & Enterprise College, Farnworth

EVIE ROGER, MISSING...

Evie Roger went missing. The police were searching for her while police officer Ben went to Evie's house to get DNA. The last time the mum saw Evie, she was wearing a red knitted jumper with dark blue jeans. Police officer Ben found Evie's thumbprint, but... there were two thumbprints and they weren't the mum's. The window was open. The other police officers found a red jumper in the forest. They went deeper into the forest and found a pair of jeans. There was a pile of leaves. They moved the pile and there was Evie Roger, dead...

Lacie-Mae Ashcroft (11)
Mount St Joseph Business & Enterprise College, Farnworth

THE VAMPIRE MYSTERY...!

Blood drained. Bites on the necks. What could it be? Dark at night, when the creature comes out of its hiding place, the mission begins. The police department searches the gloomy forest for the huge creature. *Squelch!* Sheriff Mcan steps on a body. She screams. The demon had already been out... She could catch it. The police have got suspects for what the demon could be - wolf, lion, tiger. Sheriff Mcan's father had a journal about a case like this in the 1900s. There were rumours about vampires. Are they real? Could it be a vampire?

Sienna Stratton (11)

Mount St Joseph Business & Enterprise College, Farnworth

THE MURDER SCENE

There was a murder going down. I better run so they don't find out it's me! I've got to move to another country, but how am I going to get on a plane with them knowing? I would change my identity, but they might ring the police. I'm just going to keep running and see where I go...
It's an hour later and there is a police helicopter out, so I'm just going to walk... At least I've got this COVID mask to cover my face. I'm going to get away with this.
Oh, the police are here. Goodbye...

Caitlin Lowe (12)
Mount St Joseph Business & Enterprise College, Farnworth

BLOOD LUST

Ten bodies found in the last week and they all have bite wounds on their neck. We are covering them up as animal attacks, but we all know what it is. 'Vampire'. The question is: who is the vampire?
I grin to myself. "They have no clue it's me. This is good." So, get all of your wooden stakes, put wooden bullets in your pistol and keep a lookout. It's been two weeks and they haven't found out. They are doing terrible. I walk into my office. I come out and tear every deputy open in there.

Luke Williamson (12)

Mount St Joseph Business & Enterprise College, Farnworth

UNSOLVED

A shadow at the door moved closer. I ran for the phone to call the police, but the shadow got closer to my bedroom. I screamed for my parents, but no one came. The shadow was in my bathroom now. I called the police, but the person couldn't hear me. They sent police to my house, but they couldn't find my street. The shadow was in my bedroom. I heard a creepy voice saying, "You will never escape this house." I tried to escape but my bedroom door was locked and my windows were too. Please help me!

Cassie Dann (13)
Mount St Joseph Business & Enterprise College, Farnworth

THE MURDER IN THE ATTIC

I was living in a mansion. It was big and the strange thing was, there were noises coming from the attic. I went to check, but I couldn't find the entrance to the attic. I went on the roof, there was a trapdoor. I went inside, there were a lot of bodies. My stomach turned and I vomited. I called the police.

After thirty minutes, they came. They checked everywhere, but they didn't find anything. When they left, that's when I saw *him* coming to me with a knife. Was this the end or not?

Abdul Rehman Choudhry (12)

Mount St Joseph Business & Enterprise College, Farnworth

UNSOLVED

Hello, my name is Maria. I live with my three brothers.
It started with the eldest, Zack, eighteen years old, overprotective, popular and kind; Zane, sixteen years old, popular, overprotective, nice but likes to fight; and my twin brother Michael, nerd, likes reading, is kind and a bit overprotective. Lastly, there is me, the youngest sibling out of all of them and the only girl.
When I was born, Mummy died and we lived alone, but we never found out how she died until everything changed...

Jasmine Tilson (13)
Mount St Joseph Business & Enterprise College, Farnworth

RUN

I was just on a walk when I heard a scream come from the forest. I was scared to go but I carried on, then I heard someone say, "Help!" I had to go there, so I went. I knew I was getting closer. I went deeper and deeper into the forest. The scream was getting louder. Then I saw a girl. She was tied up on a tree! I ran to her and untied her legs, she was bleeding. Suddenly, she became terrified. She was looking behind me. I looked and someone was standing behind me...

Zunaira Khan (11)
Mount St Joseph Business & Enterprise College, Farnworth

UNSOLVED

My name is Joshua. Previously, my friend went for a walk near the woods. Normally they call it Deadman's. I reported it to the police, they said, "We will try and find the missing suspect," so the police went on a hunt and they went towards the woods. But they had an eerie, mysterious feeling about what was going to happen tonight...

Mitesh Danohal (12)
Mount St Joseph Business & Enterprise College, Farnworth

HIT THE TARGET

Cracks of light outstretched into an empty night as the fury of rain soaked me. Ahead, a street light flickered orange. It was then I noticed something. A devastatingly dark figure was illuminated in the distance. It was *him*. Desperate, I accelerated towards him. Another flash of colossal lightning confirmed my suspicions. I headed left, swinging round tremendous buildings. *Crack!* A speeding bullet narrowly dodged my skull. Missing his shots, I spotted a fatal flaw. His speed was decreasing. Strategically, I slowed and took aim. His lifeless body fell limp, his unfortunate soul floating away into the sky.
He's dead.

Brandon Wingrove (13)
St Thomas More High School, Westcliff-On-Sea

GETAWAY

Electric-blue and scarlet-red lights flashed through the bank's windows while the ear-piercing sirens of twenty police cars wailed like a group of wild monkeys. Hastily, the robbers packed the lustrous clear diamonds into the duffle bag, accumulating up to £500,000,000. All of a sudden, a megaphone blasted out: "Surrender or the SWAT team will enter with force!" However, the robbers came prepared. They darted through the back door of the bank and hopped onto several getaway bikes. Bullets whizzed past the robbers' heads until one hit a duffle bag. The diamonds poured out onto the road like sparkling sand...

Sean Aboagye (14)
St Thomas More High School, Westcliff-On-Sea

"GUILTY!"

"Guilty!"
As the jury shouted, I fell onto my knees with my hands covering my head. "What? That's a massive lie! I would never do such a thing, I loved her."
"I sentence you to seventy years in prison," proclaimed the angered judge.
Two years later...
In prison, it was lunchtime and the canteen was stocked up with prison gruel. *Woo, woo!* went the alarm. There had been an escape. Police swarmed all over, the prison was overflowing.
"Everybody, get to your cells now!"
On the way to my cell, I discovered a small gap in the wall...

Owen Palmer (11)
St Thomas More High School, Westcliff-On-Sea

HIM

Something isn't right, I thought. "Guys!" They all turned and looked at me. Then I realised that they weren't looking at me, they were looking at Him. Him stood there, staring at our petrified faces, wondering who would make the first move. Michael attacked first, slicing Him in pieces scattering everywhere. Slowly, Him's body slowly began to piece back together... That's when we knew we were stuffed. It's as simple as that. As quick as a bullet, he rushed at us, flicking up all over the room, flailing. I got slammed into the wall. Instantly, I died. He killed everyone.

Oliver Nyland (13)
St Thomas More High School, Westcliff-On-Sea

COLD-HEARTED

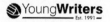

"We have ten minutes," my comrade told me. The vault stood in front of us. One barrier holding us from victory. This will be life-changing. I walked up to the lock. My hands shook. I took a deep breath, steeling myself. Placing the bomb, I quickly dialled in the detonation code. No going back now. A small beep echoed down the hallway. No explosion. My lip curled.

"The bomb doesn't work!" said my teammate.

"It never would have." A knife dropped into my hand. I embedded it into my teammate's throat. Blood stained my clothes. Betrayal tainted his pale face.

Brandon James Aguinaldo (14)
St Thomas More High School, Westcliff-On-Sea

UNSOLVED

The cold feeling of the heavy pistol in my right hand. The hands of a murderer. Today was just another day. I approached my next victim and raised my hand, took my breath and shot. *Pop! Pop! Pop!* All three bullets reached his chest. Choking on his own blood, his eyes filled with sadness and terror.
"W-why?" he gargled as his red blood seeped through his clothes.
I'm now sitting in my room as another father, son, brother, husband is taken away. Suddenly, my boss bursts into my room. "What?" I say. He glares at me.
"Your brother is dead."

Daniel Akinyeye (14)
St Thomas More High School, Westcliff-On-Sea

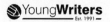

THE SLAUGHTERING

Blood splattered on the walls and ceiling, dripping like a tap, the flash of cameras blinding me, searching for clues; people wearing forensic suits, roaming around, fixed on finding an answer. Furniture upturned like a landfill site, food scattered on the floor whilst rats devoured the scraps.
I walked upstairs, hearing the officers searching for the man around the area, on the radio. I stepped into the room in search of anything belonging to the murder. I scavenged for something to find, but nothing to be seen anywhere. I turned around to look behind the door, there *he* stood...

George Sanders (14)
St Thomas More High School, Westcliff-On-Sea

BEHIND U

The suspects were gone. All that was left were nine pieces of paper on the wall. They read: 'Be careful. Even we don't know when we'll be caught. Hide while you can. I must be quiet. Nobody shall know. Don't turn back now.' The final sheet has the letter 'U' on it. Chills ran down my spine as it felt like several eyes were on me. It stood out, the capital letters of each sentence, spelling out 'Behind U'. Moments after, multiple guns clicked. Shots rang out. I fell to the floor and heard, "This investigation cannot run without you."

Mike Lagrio Pasion (13)
St Thomas More High School, Westcliff-On-Sea

BLIND KIDNAPPING

Darkness surrounded me. Voices of men in the front of the van, laughing, smirking, grinning. The seat was grubby and half torn, scratching my back. Sweat began to drip down my face as the bag continued to suffocate me. It smelled of bland coffee breath, maybe of the old victims. The car itself sounded old and rusty, the engine bellowing as the car journeyed to the unknown. Both my shoulders were gripped tightly and forcibly dragged down these crooked steps, down to the pits of death. Swiftly, the bag was taken off. The illuminating light from above immediately blinded me...

Samuel Franz Adejoro (13)
St Thomas More High School, Westcliff-On-Sea

THIEF IN THE NIGHT

It was midnight. There was no moon. It was pitch-black. Suddenly, alarms blared, lights illuminating the halls of the museum. The thief scrambled, packing the precious jewels into his dark bag. He was dressed in black. He was a shadow. He rushed down the hall, but it was too late. Police sirens echoed through the city, helicopters whirled above. They surrounded the building. Wasting no time, they entered. They scoured every part of the building. They searched it top to bottom, but the thief was nowhere to be found.
A few blocks away, a drain cover opens. He emerges...

Dawid Wisniowski (14)
St Thomas More High School, Westcliff-On-Sea

DEATH ROW

Thinking back, I shouldn't have done it. I was blackmailed. I stabbed him but there were witnesses. I felt like my heart would burst. If only they weren't there.
Twenty years later and I'm going to be killed today. I ate my last meal of a burger and Coke after saying goodbye to my friends. I walked slowly to the execution room and sat in the chair.
"Mr Matthew Hall, do you have any last words?" an officer said to me.
"I apologise to the families I affected," I answered back. I waited for the inevitable and then it happened...

David Akinyeye (14)
St Thomas More High School, Westcliff-On-Sea

THE MONEY MISSION

There I was, holding the gun to his head. *Bang!* Blood flew across the room as I packed the money and ran off to safety. As I started to lose breath, I turned into an alley. That's when I saw a shadow of a big guy. I approached him, hoping he was the one I had been looking for. It was. With a deep voice, he whispered, "Is that the £1,000,000?"
"Yes, that's all of it," I replied. "What are you doing?" I said, shaking as he held the silenced pistol to my blood-covered face.
"Next time, be quicker..."

Robert Aboagye (13)
St Thomas More High School, Westcliff-On-Sea

THE HEIST

It's one minute past midnight and we're outside one of the biggest banks in all of America. We've got our duffle bags ready, our rifles are off safety mode and we've put our masks over our heads. We're sitting in the car, waiting for the perfect time to go. We have our getaway car ready to go. I'm kind of nervous, but I know it's for the right reason. The C4's ready to blow, we'll present it at the door to blow at ten past midnight. It's time to wait.
Now it's ten past and we're waiting for the explosion...

Luke Bushby (13)
St Thomas More High School, Westcliff-On-Sea

THE CEREAL KILLER

A serial killer has been making the rounds lately. I locked the doors to my house and quietly snuck to bed. I heard glass shattering and grabbed my very large spoon. I crept downstairs and went to the sound's origin. I saw it, the serial killer! I went to bonk him with my spoon, he vanished. I looked down at the floor, my Weetabix and Cheerios lay dead on the floor. He wasn't a serial killer, he was a *cereal* killer.
It's been ten years since the incident and I haven't had cereal since. But there's always strawberry Slimfast.

Ollie Berridge (14)
St Thomas More High School, Westcliff-On-Sea

UNSOLVED

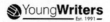

The lie detector results were back and we discovered that our detectives needed to get more training. For them to be able to train more exclusively, we had to bring out more detectives from different areas to solve different problems because there's crime every single day, and we have to be able to control our precious country and city. In order to stay safe, we have to make sure that our police, ambulances and fire engines are doing their job as they should.
Finally, our detectives are now figuring out a crime, but more crime is growing too much...

Kamsy Ugenyi (12)
St Thomas More High School, Westcliff-On-Sea

SLICE

Every Saturday, at 10am, Mrs Creme and I feed the ducks at the park, but this Saturday I felt like something was wrong. I left my house, got in the car and drove to the park. I went straight to the pond and looked at my watch, it read 9:52am. I started to get worried as she was always ten minutes early.
Fifteen minutes later, I started calling her landline. It rang, no answer. I called again, no answer. I called at least five times and then a deep voice answered.
"What?"
I said, "Mrs Creme?" and then... *slice!*

Malachi Goodrich (13)
St Thomas More High School, Westcliff-On-Sea

LIFE AS A BOUNTY HUNTER

Life as a bounty hunter requires patience and determination. I was urgently called into work, they told me they had a new lead for the case of Jefferson Daniels. He was spotted hanging around a derelict house.
Later that night, I cautiously approached the house, the windows were all smashed in. The door was ajar, so I proceeded to walk in. I was greeted by an array of blood. As I ventured into the kitchen, I noticed that a brick was sticking out. *It was a fake wall*. I heard a noise, I was being pinned down... I screamed, "Help!"

Zane Hadyaoui (13)
St Thomas More High School, Westcliff-On-Sea

THE ROBBERY

My accomplice, Tommy, shouted at the banker, ordering for them to open the safe room while holding a gun at her. Civilians were lying on the shiny granite floor, desperate to stay alive. Time was going slow as I waited to hear them sirens. The banker opened the safe room while sobbing for her life. We entered the room whilst my other accomplice, Jeremy, shouted, "Sirens!" There was a faint noise of sirens that seemed to become louder. Sweat dripped down my face as the banker attempted to open the vault, but did we have enough time to escape?

William Bolt (13)

St Thomas More High School, Westcliff-On-Sea

AUTOPSY

Some people believe in an afterlife, a second space in the same world. When I examine the dead, they show me things others can't see. My dead body for today was a male of twenty-nine. His driver's license was perfect. Yet he died in a car crash.
He had no external injuries except for a few scrapes due to the crash. However, when I dissected him, instead of finding blood clots in the coronary arteries, I saw evidence that this man was dead *before* the car crash. A burn mark in the shape of a hand surrounded his heart...

Milo Rouillion (14)
St Thomas More High School, Westcliff-On-Sea

THE MONEY HEIST

A shadow at the door... My heart pounded vigorously. Was I going to live? Who knew. An enormous bag rattled from the prisoner hijacking a bank. As soon as the suspect lay eyes on me, he escaped from my sight. Before I realised, I became a suspect for a serious crime and heist! Countlessly, I have been searching for a message to solve the crime scene. It just didn't add up, all the information the detectives gathered is all over the place. The court sent a bounty hunter to capture the criminal. Would they find him? Who knew. I wondered.

Victor Kolawole (13)
St Thomas More High School, Westcliff-On-Sea

CASE CHRONICLES: THE FIRST

It was a memorable night. I had just joined the police and was on my first case. It was a homicide. The first suspect was the victim's friend. I knocked on her door and heard glass break. I pulled out my gun and kicked down the door. She fled, the chase was on. We ran down the street, I pulled out my radio and said, "Sergeant Gerrod, I'm chasing the suspect on 4th and Reco!"
As I cornered her, gun to her head she whispered under her breath, "Bye."
As she killed herself, that was my first case closed.

Andrew Solomon-Ayoku (12)
St Thomas More High School, Westcliff-On-Sea

THE BOUNTY HUNTERS

The police failed to arrest him. Now it's our job. People call us myths, but we are the legendary bounty hunters. Whoever runs from the law deals with us. Firstly, we made plans to catch the bounty (John Morgan), his bounty was over $1000, so we had to risk everything.
Weeks later, we were ready. I gathered everyone and we all equipped ourselves with our shiny weapons and horses. We all galloped off and looked for the man who robbed the West Indian Bank but failed to run with the money. I started to worry a lot. Will I survive?

Travis Bird (13)
St Thomas More High School, Westcliff-On-Sea

THE NEIGHBOURHOOD WHERE NOTHING EVER HAPPENS

It was a neighbourhood where nothing happened, until now. It was just a casual day in the office until the TV flickered on and started playing an emergency broadcast of a mystery person. Wait, no, a mystery *thing*. It was tall and skinny with clothes splattered with blood. The figure had a misshapen head and the face was blurred. It was in a recognisable place. It was the office, the one I was in! It went dark, very dark and what felt like five minutes later, I was awoken to blood seeping from the face above. It was not human...

Joshua Milton (13)
St Thomas More High School, Westcliff-On-Sea

THE CRIMINAL KIDNAPPER

My neighbour's house is old and rickety. I knew there would be something fishy going on in there. I called the police over to the house because I had heard noises from his stuffy basement when he called me over to clean his house. Anyway, the police came and searched the house for him, but he wasn't there. What they did hear was a scuffling noise coming from the basement. They thought it was just rats, but it turned out it was full of serial killers, bounty hunters and murderers, all left to fight to the death, for some food...

Aksel Baker (12)
St Thomas More High School, Westcliff-On-Sea

ESCAPE

I am in the basement, surrounded by police. I've made a name for myself: the cannibalistic serial killer. I let them find me in the slaughterhouse. I started by making a bloodstained trail to my location. Then barricaded myself in the basement... waiting for the police to move. As the police were starting to come in, there was one exit that I created myself. An ingenious idea; only one made by a sophisticated killer like myself. Leaving my car exactly two houses down, I created a tunnel to it. My escape was a perfect plan. Bye-bye!

Sebbie Joslin (14)
St Thomas More High School, Westcliff-On-Sea

THE TESCO ROBBERY

"Guilty!"
The one word I didn't want to hear, the one word I wasn't. This case involved a Tesco robbery. I was the number-one suspect in this case as I was inside only five minutes before the crime happened. As the cold steel handcuffs were placed on my wrists, a sensation of fear and stress came over me. Thrown in the back of a grim police van which was taking me to the place I will be spending the next year of my life. This maximum-security prison would be like a living hell for an innocent man like me...

Charlie Treacher (13)
St Thomas More High School, Westcliff-On-Sea

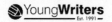

THE £400,000 HEIST

We planned the heist. It took months, but we finally did it. The heist vehicle was a Mercedes Sprinter. There were four of us on the heist. I was the driver of the van and would go in the bank first. We were aiming to steal £400,000 so we'd all have a 25% share.
Tensions built as I parked the van and once we got out, "Get down!" I yelled. Everyone in the bank screamed. A few minutes passed as I gathered up £400,000, but what I didn't realise was that it was too late. They were already onto us...

Geno Harrod (13)
St Thomas More High School, Westcliff-On-Sea

ONLY ONE

I woke up at my desk with a multitude of papers stacked up in front of me. My fellow NCCU agents were trying to figure out who had managed to tamper with the PM's secure network last night. We found leads, but they turned out to be nothing more than a group of kids playing on their computers. We traced the network for any connections and found nothing up until 1am. The screen read 'anonymous'. Only one person? We did an address check, we knew this was our guy. Then the screen read '500 known locations'. Oh no!

George Lamparter (14)
St Thomas More High School, Westcliff-On-Sea

FOOTBALL HORROR

As Coach Emerson's team started the football match, they started to play well. James, his assistant, was telling the team to get their defensive line organised, otherwise they would counter-attack and score a goal. Josh, their right-back, got the ball and tried to look for a pass. He knew that if his team did not win, they were out of the final. But then, suddenly, there was a loud bang. Three men had set off three bombs in the stadium that left many fans, players and himself (Josh) injured. That was it. His career was over.

Joshua Affen (13)
St Thomas More High School, Westcliff-On-Sea

UNSOLVED

"Guilty!" the judge said, slamming the gavel. The women were in shock. The man who cost me so much pain was going to jail for life without bail. It all started when we were both in training for nursing and were in the hospital, giving injections. Me, Johanna and Mike. Me and Mike were good friends; had a lot in common so we spent lots of time together. But then I noticed the serum was missing. I suspected Mike, but did not want to believe it. Until I found him standing over me sleeping, holding a syringe in his hand...

Tobi Awoyinfa (14)
St Thomas More High School, Westcliff-On-Sea

NIGHT-TIME DELIGHT

"Please, no, *no!*" said the officer.
"Too late," I said. As the sun went down and the moon rose up, that was our time to get in that bank. We smashed the door down, putting hot metal into anyone we saw. I went to load up my gun again, but everyone had run away. I got the password for the safe... My eyes glowed with joy, seeing stacks of gold. We jumped in excitement. We filled our bags to the max. As we were going to leave, we heard police and the SWAT team roll up. We'd really messed up...

Teddy Page (12)
St Thomas More High School, Westcliff-On-Sea

HOMELESS OR CRIMINAL?

The suspect was gone. We couldn't catch him. We drove around the city for hours, searching for cameras or any evidence that could be of any use. Midnight was quickly approaching and we were about to give up and head home when something caught my eye. It was a man sitting on the sidewalk, staring directly at the crime scene. How had we not spotted him earlier when we patrolled around the building? We slowly edged closer to ask him if he had seen anyone leave, he said he had seen a man dressed in black go down an alley...

William James Love (14)
St Thomas More High School, Westcliff-On-Sea

UNKNOWN

Running, I swiftly turned my head to check if *it* was gone. So many questions. Where did it go? Who is it? I slowed down, confused at where it went. The rain surrounded me as if it was a tsunami. Scared, I shivered in fear and turned around, all alone. They left me here. Not knowing where I was, fog seemed to trap me in a box, cutting out all my surroundings. A twig snapped. Checking all around me, sweat dripped from my hair. Continuing to run, I tripped over a log.
It was coming. Jumping out at me. Devoured.

Edward Fenn (14)

St Thomas More High School, Westcliff-On-Sea

A SHADOW, A GHOST

A shadow, a ghost. That's what they called the killer. There was no DNA, no description of the killer. The only thing that was left was the murder tool and a tape. The killer just repeated a series of numbers. Nobody could figure out what the numbers meant.

The case broke me, there was no way of fixing me. I still have to go to therapy, even though the murders were twenty years ago. It was a cold case from way back when it began. No one could solve this case. Sometimes I think the killer is my own shadow...

Louis Dowman (14)
St Thomas More High School, Westcliff-On-Sea

THE RETURN...

It was a case I was given in my first year as a detective, and recently there has been some chat about him returning. I had chased him for two years before he just disappeared. As soon as I heard this, I quickly took the case back on and looked over the evidence, however, there was nothing. No photos, no evidence at all. I looked around and asked around, but since it was an inactive case, there was nothing until I heard the *ching* of a knife and the subtle snickering of a man I knew too well behind me...

James Watchorn (14)
St Thomas More High School, Westcliff-On-Sea

UNSOLVED

It just didn't add up. How had I been found this soon? I had to gather all my resources as fast as I could. I picked up the pace as I heard the military pull up. I put my suit on and jumped off the twelve-storey building. The origin of the manmade virus hadn't been discovered after months of searching and being framed. Where did it come from, who released it, why does it control people? An unsolved crime that hopefully I will find to clear my name. It remains the mystery of the Manmade Controller Virus.

Tamlin Dean (14)

St Thomas More High School, Westcliff-On-Sea

TERROR IN LONDON

I still remember, to this day, the tremendous thing that happened! I was in the busy streets of London when, all of a sudden, an explosion occurred. I was with my friends, so we all ran. I glanced back and I heard gunshots. They were very loud and I was frightened. I got behind an abandoned car, there were bullets flying over my head like an angry rain cloud. I saw many of my friends and other people getting shot to the ground. All of a sudden, I saw my life flash before my eyes. Red stained my white shirt...

Maximilian Rodger (12)
St Thomas More High School, Westcliff-On-Sea

IT WASN'T ME

"Guilty!"
I fell to my knees, I heard the cries of my family. It was him, the man in black, that bloodthirsty moron. I was trying to protect my family; he put a gun to my mother's head. He told me he would leave if I gave him my school's address and, foolishly, I did. He killed them, he killed them all! The judge told security to take me away, I felt the anger the parents threw at me. I vowed to kill him no matter the cost. This was the last thing before rage would swallow me whole.

Aaron Wole-Romiluyi (13)
St Thomas More High School, Westcliff-On-Sea

THE HUNT

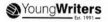

It had been three days since the trial finished, but there was more evidence found, and we had been informed that the secretive suspect was on the run and he plus other hunters were dispatched. This new evidence was part of the old case during the trial, another piece of the puzzle. The man was spotted on the edge of a bridge with a woman and had demanded money, so all of the police force were trying to negotiate, but he kept getting closer to the edge...
"Goodbye," he said. After, he jumped...

Lukas Beniusis (12)
St Thomas More High School, Westcliff-On-Sea

DRONE SCHEMATICS

I looked from left to right, then I made a dash for the facility. There was a guard, I silently executed him for his keycard and then shrouded the body. I slowly pulled my drone out of my duffle bag and set it down to the ground, and then took flight. I was trying to navigate my way into the main vents, but they were one step ahead of me and had barred it off. Then I used my keycard and entered through the main entrance and started running, trying not to get found. Then I stole the schematics...

Joe Sheehan (12)
St Thomas More High School, Westcliff-On-Sea

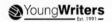

THE CAYO PERICO HEIST

A shadow at the door... I got closer to the shadow in my submarine, it was an underwater mine. I had to dodge them. When I got to the island, there were loads of security guards and cameras. I had to take them out quietly. I hoped I didn't get caught by the sightseeing cameras. I needed to be quick to get the keycards to the vault, there were loads of gold bars in the vault. I was living the dream.
In an emergency, I had to get back to my submarine just in case I got caught by guards.

Lewis Wilson (14)
St Thomas More High School, Westcliff-On-Sea

SUSPICIOUS

Today was a day like any other. The sun rose from its white blanket and I steadily left my imagery. Realising that I was awake, I got changed, raced towards the door and quickly sat in the wine-red car, heading to work. When I turned right on the main road, I realised that a huge black van had been behind me ever since I left the house. I suspected a trail was on me, so to convince myself, I turned into a cramped street. As the van appeared, blocking the entrance, an armed man aimed at me...

Danil Biriulynas (12)
St Thomas More High School, Westcliff-On-Sea

UNSOLVED

My eyes glazed over the laptop, dry and weary from overworking. The monotone blue buzz becoming a regular appearance now since work became sparse and few and far between. My line of work is quite gruesome and lonely. *Ding!* I fell off my seat, surprised at the sudden noise. There it was, a job! I read over it, an open and shut assassination of a not-so-loyal husband. I prepared, reloading my weapons, and opened the door, bathing in the fresh air. Let the hunt begin.

Isaac Nai (14)

St Thomas More High School, Westcliff-On-Sea

THE MYSTERY

It just didn't add up. I went to the house where the Evans family had been murdered. I found a few drops of blood, no bodies. There was a note on the door saying: 'This may not add up now but it will add up at the end. Go to the thing that is closest to your heart'. "Family." I rushed back home and the door was opened and the handle was broken. My dog, Benji, was barking and was upstairs. I went upstairs and in my room was the murderer. It adds up...

Danny Crotty (13)
St Thomas More High School, Westcliff-On-Sea

THE BODY!

"Hello?" I shouted. It was 3am, I was down by the local river. The bag I was dragging, a black bag, felt like I was carrying a thousand things on my back. The street lamps barely lit the dark water of the river. As I was lowering the body into the river, I heard a scream. A woman was walking her small dog on the other side of the river. I dropped the body and ran out the park, back towards my small flat.
Had I gotten away with it? Would the police come for me?

Monty Crabb (13)
St Thomas More High School, Westcliff-On-Sea

THE GANG

Bang, bang, bang! and he went down like a ton of bricks. He ran until he couldn't run anymore.
"We are the leaders of the gang, H1, H2, H3. We have five thousand and seven hundred in our gang!" they shouted. H1 shouted to H2, "We want to go soon." H2 replied, "We almost got caught." They heard footsteps on the ground getting closer and closer. "Quick! Run, we need to run and start a new life in Texas!" H2 shouted. H2 and H1 began to carry H3 who was bleeding from his thigh.
"Quick! He's there!" H1 shouted...

Bailey Dobson (14)
Stephenson Academy, Stantonbury

A BODY FOUND IN THE FOREST

The sky started turning pitch-black, grey gloomy clouds swirled as the wind blew with great force, turning my pale warm skin to ice. The sounds of dead crispy leaves crunching became louder as my shoes stepped on each one. My teeth started chattering uncontrollably like an alarm clock, and my eyes weren't focused as I was looking around the harrowing forest. Butterflies started forming, fluttering in my stomach. I went deeper, then I tripped... My whole body fell onto the damp ground and the thing that made me trip wasn't some large log... It was a dead body. I froze.

Sarah Okor (15)
Stephenson Academy, Stantonbury

THE CCTV CAMERA

As I slowly turned to my left, I saw a shadow at the door, then it became two, then three, then four. The moment I had been dreading unfolding right in front of me. Four masked men, guns drawn, came running into the bank, demanding money.
I just wish this stupid system would let me learn quicker. They seemed very professional, as if this wasn't their first bank robbery. I switched to my other camera, the outside one so I could get a picture of the van's number plate. *Dun, dun!* My cameras crashed! I was hacked... Everything went black...

Ben Garner (15)
Stephenson Academy, Stantonbury

SURVIVOR OF TORTURE

A shadow at the door made me paranoid. I had just woken up in a strange place that I have never seen before! There were chains on my arms and legs. I scanned the mysterious room, I detected a timer on the wall with one minute left on it. There was a remarkably rusty chainsaw in the corner. I grappled for the chainsaw. It wouldn't turn on. Time was running out. Finally, it started. I carved the chains off. I cut the hinges off the door and rapidly ran outside. Will they ever catch the vile person who did this?

Levi Cinqermani (15)
Stephenson Academy, Stantonbury

1976

I was walking in the streets. I'm a detective, my name is Tyler Eaton. Then I saw a dead body. I was shocked. I saw someone near it with a mask. He ran away. I'll find him.
The next morning, I was visited by Mike. "Do you know who it was?" he said.
"No," I said.
"Hold my bag," and I did. I heard a tool in the bag. I opened it and I was shocked. It was the mask from last night and a knife with it! I called the police. That was the last time I saw him.

Tyler Easton (13)
Stephenson Academy, Stantonbury

THE BOMBING

You may start when ready. Make sure you two teams and the sniper show no mercy to the people who rob our people and mass kill our people. Our country has been bankrupt for years because of them. Today we take it into our hands. We kill their president with 5.56s and bombs.
Team One, plate the C4 under the armed guards. Team Two, guns ready. Sniper, you know what to do. Three, two, one, go! After, go to the van in the side street. In the van are new clothes and IDs for a way out of this mess!

Alex de Quincey (15)
Stephenson Academy, Stantonbury

WHY?

I hear the echo of the bell as I leave English and head to my dorm room. As my door opens, it squeaks. I hear a boom and screams. I look out the window and see a man wearing a black mask shooting students dead! I'm scared for my life as the man in the black mask sees me looking. The man shoots at me, but I duck just in time. The glass shatters on top of me. I cut my hands on the glass as I struggle to leave the room. I feel shocked that someone would do that!

Alfie Ward (15)
Stephenson Academy, Stantonbury

MYSTERY DETECTIVE

I blacked out in court. The footprints weren't hers. They were Sheriff Johns'. The teacher was innocent. She bought cookies from Sheriff Johns. He was the man. I'd found evidence. You see, there was one glove in Johns' coat. I found the other one behind the bushes in the place and it was his DNA.

But the killer *was* the teacher.

I woke up, not remembering anything. She grabbed the gun from my jeans. "You fools! I played you! I got Johns' stuff and placed it everywhere." The only one who knew was Detective Eda.

"Teacher, stop!"

The window opened...

Rama AlmuTairi (14)

Ummul Mumineen Academy, Grangetown

COLD CASE

I killed her! She's gone and no one can know. I washed my hands and headed to work. I walked into work and there, on the screen, was a man bearing an uncanny resemblance to me. My colleague, John, gave me a look and said, "Looks like you, huh?"

"A lot of people look like me."

I knew my next victims.

On the news: "Two FBI agents have been found dead, horribly mutilated. Don Truman and John Michael were murdered. These are the third murders in a week. Ava Lennon was also murdered. Their families are yet to comment."

Humayra Arish (13)
Ummul Mumineen Academy, Grangetown

TRACING THE DEPTHS

He was left there, dead. The room was cold, airy and nothing felt right. A party had been crashed by a murder and break-in. The suspect had vanished and all CCTV was gone. He must've had an accomplice. All the people at the party had been taken into custody. They all told a different story, saving themselves. The victim had no link to the suspect. It was sudden, out of the blue. There was no lead, nowhere to start. Until something disturbing was found. Someone had carved their initials into the impeachable victim's legs. Everyone was shocked...

Hannah Ebrahim (13)

Ummul Mumineen Academy, Grangetown

I'M INNOCENT!

It just didn't add up. All I was doing was getting my lunch until my eye caught something - it was a pocketknife. I didn't think anything of it until I realised... I don't own a knife! This wasn't my bag! The knife was wrapped in a white piece of kitchen towel and was covered in dry blood. I had to leave before anyone found out about this!
I haven't been to work since then. I can't tell anyone why! What if I'm being framed? Who would do this? Maybe my manager, he's been awfully nice to me recently...

Iffat Ahmed (12)
Ummul Mumineen Academy, Grangetown

AT THE DOORSTEP

People think that the dead can't talk. I, Detective Adam, was called in to the station as there was an eyewitness for a boy who had gotten in a car accident two years ago. The report was from a mother called Rosa. It was her cousin. She told me that it all happened when he had a call from a friend who asked him to hang out. He was on his way but got hit and died. He was a twenty-three-year-old and appeared at Rosa's doorstep out of nowhere, so she phoned us. To be continued...

Maliha Haq (11)

Ummul Mumineen Academy, Grangetown

YOUNG WRITERS INFORMATION

We hope you have enjoyed reading this book – and that you will continue to in the coming years.

If you're a young writer who enjoys reading and creative writing, or the parent of an enthusiastic poet or story writer, visit our website **www.youngwriters.co.uk/subscribe** to join the World of Young Writers and receive news, competitions, writing challenges, tips, articles and giveaways! There is lots to keep budding writers motivated to write!

If you would like to order further copies of this book, or any of our other titles, then please give us a call or order via your online account.

Young Writers
Remus House
Coltsfoot Drive
Peterborough
PE2 9BF
(01733) 890066
info@youngwriters.co.uk

Join in the conversation!
Tips, news, giveaways and much more!

 YoungWritersUK  @YoungWritersCW  YoungWritersCW